The Awkward Owl

Flying Basics:
For the Beginner Bird

$24.99

By Dr. O. W. Learner, Ph.D.

In depth coverage with diagrams on topics such as:
1. How to go up
2. How to go down
3. Object avoidance
4. Wing exercises
5. Proper landing procedures
6. Creating flight plans
7. Migration do's and don'ts
8. Emergency landings

Byrd Press, Inc., Migration City, Missouri, USA

written & illustrated by Shawnda Blake

Awkward Owl Readers

Awkward Owl Media, LLC
www.AwkwardOwlReaders.com

Copyright Page
Illustration by:
Alex

For Evan, Lauren & Alex

Especially for Lauren who inspired this book, even though what she really saw was a turkey vulture.

An **Awkward Owl Reader**, a publication of **Awkward Owl Media, LLC**.

For more information go to **www.AwkwardOwlReaders.com**

Once there was an
awkward owl.

While other owls
could swoop,

and soar...

the awkward owl
could only flop

and flail.

In fact, he was
SO awkward...

people would point
and say, "_Well_, would
you look at _that_. What
an AWKWARD owl!"

Which, of course,
makes an awkward owl
even MORE awkward.

back-side

bottom-side

One day, the
awkward owl flew
back-side-up
and **bottom-side-first**,
SMACK,
into a big oak tree.

A little girl saw him fall
to the ground and asked,
*"Poor little thing,
are you hurt?"*

The awkward owl could only say "*Who, Who?*", which made the little girl smile, "*Why, you!*"

She gently scooped
him up, and carried
him into her house,
where her mom said...

"GET THAT THING
OUT OF THE KITCHEN!"

So she did.

Her mom helped her
fix a place for the
awkward owl to sleep...
outside.

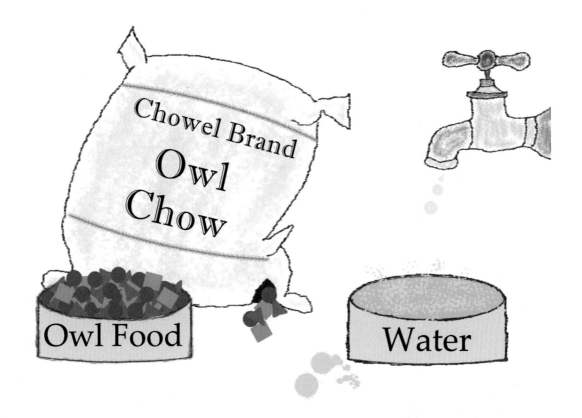

The little girl took very good care of the little owl.

She loved the little owl
and worried because
he did not fly.

Soon the little owl began
to love her too, and he
decided to give it a try.

So he slowly
s-t-r-e-t-c-h-e-d
his wings and
got ready to fly.

He was EXPECTING to fly back-side-up and bottom-side-first, but just as he flapped his wings, the little girl whispered *"You can do it!"*.

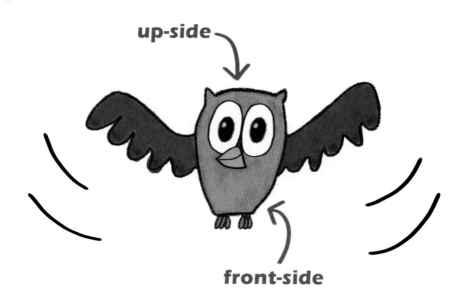

up-side

front-side

And INSTEAD, he flew
UP-side-up and
FRONT-side-first
UP into the air.

He could swoop.

He could soar!

He gracefully flew...

to the big oak tree in the little girl's yard,

where he decided to stay.

And now, at the end of each day, just before saying "*Good Night!*", the girl asks, "*Who's my favorite owl?*".

Of course, the owl can STILL only say "*Who?*", and so every night, as she turns off the light, the girl says with a smile, "*Why YOU!*".

Improved! More Mouse Flavor!

Hoot SWeetS

Gluten Free!

OWL Treats

For the WiSe OWL

Allergy Warning: May contain insect pieces. Do NOT eat if insects bug you.

TO:
My Favorite Owl

Birds of a feather
wash together

FOWL
OWL

Feather Wash

The End

AWKWARD OWL READERS

Being awkward makes life hard for a little owl learning to fly. While all the other owls swoop and soar, the awkward owl ends up crashing into a big oak tree. Will he ever get the confidence he needs to take to the skies?

Emma Marie wants a pet more than ANYTHING, but convincing Mom is not easy! Then disaster strikes when her new turtle starts sneezing, LOUDLY.

Will her Mom let her keep such a noisy pet?

You'll never guess how things turn out in this illustrated, rhyming book for children. Then meet the turtle who inspired the story!

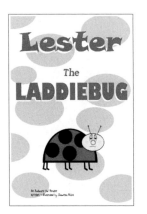

Lester the ladybug is tired of being teased by all the other bugs. He has tried everything but none of his remedies has helped. It is not until he meets another ladybug that he realizes…maybe he doesn't need to change at all.

Do you want to learn how to make the best pie in the world? This illustrated picture book reveals the top-secret, highly classified recipe for making the most amazing and delicious Snootenberry pie.

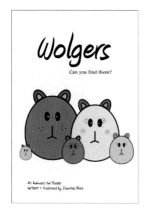

Where are all the Wolgers? Wolgers are small and cute and round and VERY good at hiding. Can you find them in this illustrated, look-and-find book?

Kids won't even know you are introducing them to prepositions needed for early language development...and DON'T tell them!

An imaginative look at the yearly Christmas tradition of the gingerbread house, Ginger's New House tells about a gingerbread girl whose family is ready to move. They just have to wait for the construction workers and decorators to finish!

Awkward Owl Media, LLC
www.AwkwardOwlReaders.com

Made in the USA
San Bernardino, CA
04 December 2015